Honeypot Hill

To the City

Saffron Thimble's Sewing Shop

The Orchards

Paddle Steamer Quay

Aunt Marigold's General Store

Lavender Valley Garden Centre

Healing House and Garden

The Worthingtons' House

Lavender Lake

Bumble Bee's Teashop

Lavender Lake School of Dance

Hedgerows Hotel
Where Mimosa lives

SCHOOL

Peppermint Pond

Rosehip School

Summer Meadow

Christmas Corner

Wildspice Woods

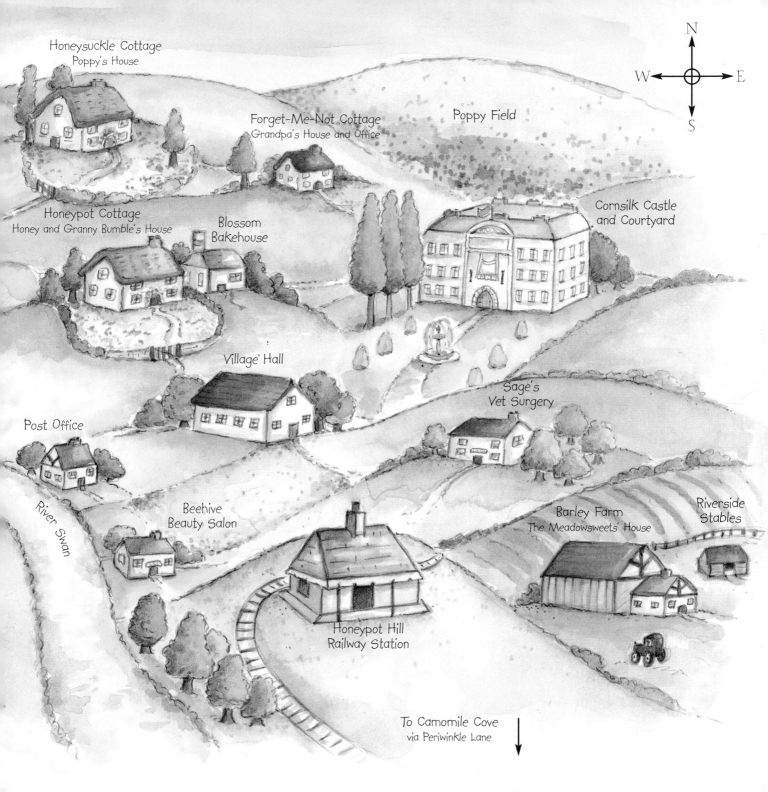

Honeysuckle Cottage
Poppy's House

Forget-Me-Not Cottage
Grandpa's House and Office

Poppy Field

N
W   E
S

Cornsilk Castle
and Courtyard

Honeypot Cottage
Honey and Granny Bumble's House

Blossom
Bakehouse

Village Hall

Sage's
Vet Surgery

Post Office

Beehive
Beauty Salon

Barley Farm
The Meadowsweets' House

Riverside
Stables

River Swan

Honeypot Hill
Railway Station

To Camomile Cove
via Periwinkle Lane

Join Princess Poppy on more adventures . . .

★ The Birthday (also available as a book and CD) ★

★ The Fair Day Ball (also available as a book and CD) ★

★ Twinkletoes (also available as abook and CD) ★

★ The Wedding ★ The Play ★ Poppy's Secret Christmas ★ The Baby Twins ★

★ Friends Together ★ Petals and Picnics - A Make-and-Do Book ★

★ Puzzle and Play - A Sticker Activity Book ★ A True Princess ★ Pocket Money Princess ★

★ The Haunted Holiday ★ The Big Mix-Up ★

BALLET SHOES
A PICTURE CORGI BOOK: 978 0 552 55664 4

First published in Great Britain by Picture Corgi,
an imprint of Random House Children's Books

This edition published 2007

3 5 7 9 10 8 6 4

Text copyright © Janey Louise Jones, 2006
Illustration copyright © Picture Corgi Books, 2006
Design by Tracey Cunnell

Picture Corgi Books are published by Random House Children's Books, London, Sydney,
Auckland, Johannesburg, New Delhi and agencies throughout the world.

THE RANDOM HOUSE GROUP Limited Reg. No. 954009
www.kidsatrandomhouse.co.uk
www.princesspoppy.com

A CIP catalogue record for this book is available from the British Library.

Printed in China

Princess Poppy

Ballet Shoes

Written by Janey Louise Jones

PICTURE CORGI

For Katie Molly,
who loves to dance

★

Ballet Shoes

featuring

Honey
★

Grandpa
★

Mum
★

Mimosa
★

Princess Poppy

Granny Bumble
★

Madame Angelwing
★

The glass doors of the sitting room at Honeysuckle Cottage were open to the garden. Poppy danced and floated around the sunlit room.

"My new ballet shoes are a perfect fit, Mum!" she called.

Poppy pointed her toes, held onto the sofa as a barre and practised her foot positions. She did a pirouette, and then curtsied to her audience of nodding flowers in the garden beyond!

"Madame Angelwing is choosing parts for the Big Show today," Poppy told her mum. "I just know I'm going to be Coppelia — a living, dancing doll!" she said.

"Don't be too sure," warned Mum, worried that Poppy would be disappointed if she wasn't picked. "The person who dances the best on the day will be chosen."

"It has to be me," laughed Poppy. "I'm the best dancer by far! *And* cousin Saffron is going to make me my own beautiful Coppelia dress!"

As they were leaving for the audition, Poppy saw that her best friend Honey was at the garden gate.

"Honey, why don't you come to ballet with me?" called Poppy. "Madame Angelwing needs some extra villagers for the street scene in *Coppelia!*"

Honey had never been to ballet before.

"Well, you do love to dance, don't you, Honey?" said Granny Bumble.

"I do," Honey said, and dashed off in the direction of her house to find something pretty to wear to her first ballet class.

They arrived at the Lavender Lake School of Dance and found Madame Angelwing in a very excited state.

"*Doucement!*" she called to the pianist, who was playing too quickly.

"*Arabesque*, not *jeté*!" she cried to an older girl in a pink leotard.

Honey thought this was all very strange and a bit scary too! But she did love the way the dancers moved so gracefully across the floor.

"Poppy!" said the teacher, clapping
her hands quickly above her head.
"Dance for me! Now!"

Poppy wasn't at all nervous,
and she began to twirl . . .

and jump, just as she had practised
in her own sitting room.

"Bravo, bravo!" cried Madame, clapping. "And who is this new girl?" she asked, looking at Honey.

"I . . . I . . . I'm Honey," stammered Honey, looking a bit red and scared.

"Well, Honey, let me see you dance!" demanded Madame Angelwing.

Honey began to glide
across the dance floor.

She moved like a fairy
flittering around on
light, silky wings.

Everyone fell silent as they watched
her dainty jumps and spins.

Madame glided across the dance floor to Honey and stood by the barre. "Honey, you move like a natural dancer. You, child, will dance Coppelia!" she announced.

Poppy's mouth dropped open in amazement. But Honey was *only* meant to be a villager! "I should be Coppelia – I *am* Coppelia!" thought Poppy, furiously.

Mum put an arm around Poppy. "Let's go and say 'Well done' to Honey, shall we?" she suggested.

But Poppy couldn't. She burst into tears of anger and disappointment . . . and something else . . . it was a feeling that she couldn't understand. She was annoyed with herself for bringing Honey along to *her* ballet class.

For the next few days, Poppy refused to play with Honey.
Instead she imagined that her dolls and toys had come to life,
just like the doll in the story of *Coppelia*.

"You would never steal my part in a show, would you, Ruby?"
she said to her big rag doll.

Poppy felt even worse when she looked over her garden gate and saw Honey playing with a new friend, Mimosa, whose parents owned the Hedgerows Hotel in Honeypot Hill.

It was bad enough to lose the part of Coppelia, but to lose her best friend was unbearable!

When Grandpa came round, Poppy flung her arms around him and cried. She cried about the ballet show, but mostly she cried because she missed Honey.

"Poppy," said Grandpa, "you will always be my little star. But you can't *always* be the star of the show. You are my Princess Poppy, and to be a true princess you need to be kind and generous to your friends."

"I *do* miss Honey," sniffed Poppy.

"And Honey misses you," said Grandpa. "Why don't you go and make friends with her again?"

But the next day at ballet class, Poppy was surprised to find that Honey wasn't there.

"Girls," said Madame, "Honey has a bad tummy ache, so she cannot dance the part of Coppelia. Instead, the Coppelia for tomorrow's Big Show will be . . . Mademoiselle Poppy!"

Poppy was thrilled! She couldn't believe it!

But then she thought about Honey, and how disappointed she would
be not to dance in the show.

"Mum, could I take some flowers to Honey?" Poppy asked after class.
"I'm sure they would make her feel better."

"What a lovely idea," said Poppy's mum.

"POPPY!" squealed Honey with delight, as her friend came into her room.

Poppy smiled and handed the flowers to Honey.

"Honey, I think you would have been a lovely Coppelia," said Poppy. "Oh, I wish you were well enough to dance the part."

Honey gave Poppy a big hug.

And all of a sudden . . . Honey felt much better!

Honey felt well enough to dance Coppelia at the Big Show.
And she danced it beautifully. Everyone said that she
was the most graceful ballerina they had ever seen.

Poppy danced the part of Swanhilde, wearing satin shoes and a beautiful pink tutu made especially for her by Saffron. Everyone clapped as Poppy twirled lightly around the stage.

At the end of the show Honey was
given a posy of sweet-smelling flowers.
She broke open the posy and gave half
of it to Poppy. They curtsied together
and hugged, glad to be friends again.

After the show, Grandpa came backstage. "Poppy, you were wonderful!" he told her.

"Oh, thank you, Grandpa! I'm so glad I made a good job of my part. Even though it was smaller than Honey's, I was still important in the story, wasn't I?" asked Poppy.

"Darling, there wouldn't have been a story, without you," replied Grandpa. "My little ballerina Princess Poppy!"